About this book

Many children have difficulty puzzling out letters because they
are abstract symbols. Letterland's worldwide success is all about its
enduring characters who give these symbols life and stop them from
being abstract. In this book we meet Ticking Tess. Her story is carefully
designed to emphasise the sounds that the letter 'T' makes in words.
This definitive, original story book is an instant collector's classic,
making learning fun for a new generation of readers.

A TEMPLAR BOOK

This edition published in the UK in 2008 by Templar Publishing
an imprint of The Templar Company plc,
The Granary, North Street, Dorking, Surrey, RH4 1DN, UK
www.templarco.co.uk

First published by Thomas Nelson & Sons Ltd, 1993
Devised and produced by The Templar Company plc

ISBN 978-1-84011-767-7

Printed in China

Letterland © was devised by and is the copyright of Lyn Wendon
LETTERLAND® is a registered trademark

Classic LETTERLAND
Storybooks

Ticking Tess and the Tiger

Written by Stephanie Laslett

Illustrated by
Jane Launchbury

templar publishing

Ticking Tess was in a terrible temper. She had made a nice treacle tart and put it out to cool on a tray in the garden. But when she went back to get it, her beautiful tart had teeth marks in it!

From the tower Ticking Tess telephoned Clever Cat to tell her what had happened.
"That is very strange," said Clever Cat. "I left a lovely cream cake on the windowsill yesterday and someone took a bite out of it. The same thing happened to some buns Bouncy Ben baked – *and* to Dippy Duck's doughnuts. Whoever can it be?"

"I can't think," said Ticking Tess.

Ticking Tess put down the telephone. She was just starting to tidy up the Telecom Tower when a sudden noise made her jump.

It was her teletouch transmitter. "Ticker, ticker, ticker, ticker!" it went as it printed out a message.

"DANGER! BEWARE!" read Ticking Tess. "Escaped tiger loose in Letterland! Please tell all Letterlanders to take great care!"

Ticking Tess trembled. "A tiger on the loose! How terrible! I must telephone everyone at once and tell them the news."

The first person Ticking Tess telephoned was her team mate Ticking Tom. He was setting up a new radar dish on a nearby tower block.

As Tess spoke she heard a loud roar outside and saw a stripy tail disappearing behind a tree. What's more, there was now a huge bite missing from her treacle tart.

"Oh dear! The tiger is here!" she said down the telephone to Ticking Tom. "Whatever shall I do?"
"I'll be there in two ticks," he said.

Soon Ticking Tom arrived. Clever Cat and Bouncy Ben were with him.

"Don't worry," said Tom. "We have a plan to catch the tiger in a special trap. I have all the tools here to build one."

"Terrific!" said Ticking Tess. "But please don't build it *too* near the tower."

First Ticking Tom dug a huge hole. Then he stretched a tarpaulin over the top. Finally Bouncy Ben covered the tarpaulin with twigs.

"We need something tasty to tempt the tiger," said Clever Cat.

"How about some treacle tart!" said Ticking Tess. "I think this tiger may have a sweet tooth!"

All night long the four friends took turn keeping watch on the tiger trap. But Bouncy Ben was so tired that he fell asleep during his turn.

He woke with a start to the sound of birds singing. It was morning! "Wake up everyone!" he cried. "We must inspect the trap!"

Ticking Tom led the way as they all tiptoed to the bottom of the garden. There was something in the trap.

It didn't have stripes.
It didn't have whiskers.
And it certainly wasn't terrible…

WITHDRAWN

"It's Todd Turtle!" cried Bouncy Ben. "What's going on?" muttered the turtle as they pulled him out. "I was just taking a stroll when I tripped into a trap… terrible shock… jolly tasty treacle, though."

Ticking Tom repaired the trap. This time Ticking Tess put some toffee in to tempt the tiger.

That afternoon the friends went inside to watch television. After a while they heard a loud noise. "Quick!" cried Clever Cat. Something was in the trap – and it was in a terrific temper. But it didn't sound like a tiger…

"Gobble, gobble, gobble, gobble, squaaark!" it went. Timidly, Ticking Tess and her friends peered inside the trap.

"It's my friend, Terence Turkey," laughed Bouncy Ben as they lifted him out. "He lives on the farm."
"I am sorry," said Ticking Tess, but the turkey was so cross he could hardly talk.

"Are you *sure* you saw a tiger?" asked Clever Cat.
"Yes, of course I did!" replied Ticking Tess, looking hot and bothered.
"We'll just try one more time," said Clever Cat.

That night Ticking Tess had terrible dreams, full of tigers twirling their tails and twitching their whiskers. She could hear their terrifying roars in her sleep…

Suddenly, she was wide awake. She *could* hear a tiger! A screeching, growling sound – a terrible sound! Something was waving its tail through a hole in the trap. It had brown and yellow stripes. It was a tiger tail!

"Come quickly!" cried Ticking Tess. "We've caught the tiger!"
They tiptoed down to the trap.
Can you guess what they had caught?

It wasn't the tiger. It was Tabitha the tabby cat. She was in a terrible temper and they had to give her ten tasty fish titbits to cheer her up.

"Was it you who tasted my treacle tart?" asked Ticking Tess.
"Or my cream cake?" said Clever Cat.
"No, no, no!" cried Tabitha. "It was not me. I hate cake. I only like fish!"

"Well, who was it then?" cried Ticking Tom. But before anyone could answer a deep voice behind them growled.
"It was me, I'm afraid." And there behind them was the hugest, stripiest tiger they had ever seen.

"It's the tiger! It's the tiger!" they cried and ran away as fast as they could. All except for Ticking Tess who was too frightened even to move. But to her surprise, the tiger wasn't at all fierce.

"I'm truly sorry," he said timidly. "I thought you had left those tempting treats out for me."

"No, I did not!" cried Ticking Tess.

"How terrible!" said the tiger. "I would never have tasted them if I had known. To tell you the truth, I don't much like cakes anyway."

Ticking Tess burst out laughing and patted the tiger on the head.

"Don't worry," she said. "I'm sure I can find you something else to eat."

Soon Ticking Tess and the tiger were sitting down to afternoon tea. Ticking Tess had tomato sandwiches and treacle tart. The tiger had some of Tabitha's fishy titbits. "Delicious!" he purred, popping one into his mouth.

Clever Cat, Ticking Tom and Bouncy Ben couldn't believe their eyes when they returned.
"Crumbs!" said Clever Cat. "Ticking Tess has tamed the tiger!"

And after that can you guess what they called Tess? Why, Ticking Tess the Tiger Tamer, of course.

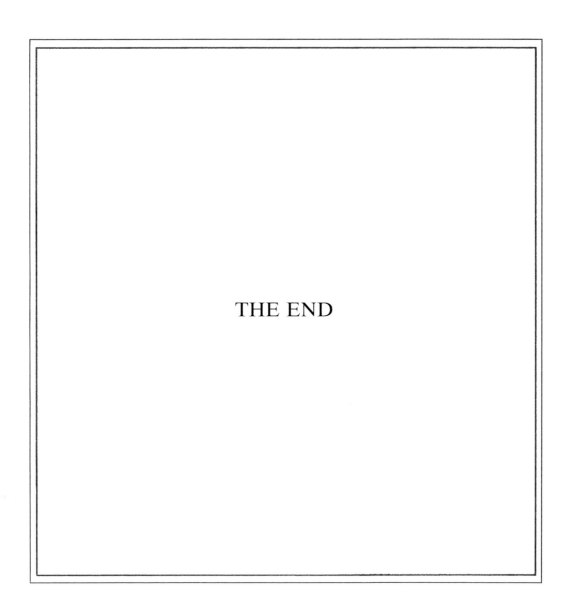

THE END